# A DEEWANA GOT ME

## KATRINA

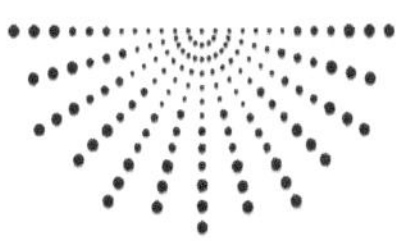

### JUST BAE

ISBN: 978-1-925988-49-9

# CONTENTS

# PROLOGUE

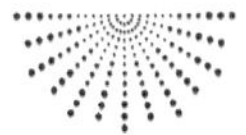

On a warm evening Katrina and Giri sat facing each other. It was the most unromantic environment and Giri chose that rather inauspicious moment to open his heart. He glanced down at Katrina's rounded breasts just above the table and quickly shifted his gaze as she looked.

"I always admired you from the time I was about ten and you were fourteen." Giri pondered. "You had such beautiful eyes and I saw you smiled often but spoke little."

Slightly embarrassed, Katrina tried to reminisce those days in that small village in India.

"You were always on my mind." Giri continued. "Years later, I am heartbroken because you married."

Being the perceptive woman she was, Katrina wasn't fazed. She was perhaps a bit surprised that Giri would admit that. She saw his eyes wandering over her body. The present declaration was serious because now he was a high-ranking official in the Central Government.

Flash back almost twenty years ago, Katrina, pictured that scene where she played on the dirt streets of Devi Nagar and vaguely recollected Giri as a little girl. Nowadays, he still has some of his boyish charm as mentioned by some of Katrina's friends who also work in the Central Government and some under Giri.

There was an incident in Katrina's marriage three years ago, where Giri was briefly featured. It was during a weekend trip to a resort with her husband, Anil. Katrina and her hubby were tucking themselves into bed on a cool night. His arms was around her waist and Anil kissed his wife on the forehead.

"Wow! That Giri is simply crazy about you." Anil began.

"Why? What happened?"

"No, of course not. He would never say such a thing to me. I'd beat his ass."

"Baby, you are so funny."

"I saw him checking you out. All in every curve in the jeans you had on."

"Oh, really. I won't wear them again." Katrina snuggled closer to Anil. "Are you upset?"

"No! Just the opposite. It actually turns me on!"

"You freak? How?" Katrina looked into Anil's eyes for answers.

"It's good to know other men are craving for my love! I love that feeling of having you while they can't."

"That's weird." Katrina pondered. "Do you like him looking at me like that?"

"I know you don't understand, sweetheart, but that's how a man's brain works sometimes." Anil moved closer as his dick pushed up against his pajamas and Katrina felt it. She turned back expecting a full thrust momentarily.

Anil moved over lowering his pajamas to bring out his throbbing love stick and Katrina simultaneously lifted her nightie and opened her thighs. She held his dick and stroked it up and down her hairy lips a few times. The quickness with which she could get herself wet was amazing. Anil slipped in with ease and then went onto a smooth rhythm that only couples know.

"Do me a favour, sweetie." Anil interrupted. "Imagine that Giri's fucking you."

"No, and why?" She shook her head stopping her bodily reciprocation.

"My love, this is just a fantasy." Anil's strokes became stronger and deeper. "I want to be him today and I want you to play along. I can be someone else for a change. That guy's lonely and he wants you. Give in to him a least once."

Katrina didn't answer but her participation returned feeling aroused by Anil's suggestion. Anil thrusted into her pussy with energy panting and gasping.

"I saw him in a nightclub's dressing room once. He's not big but good looking." Anil slowed down.

Katrina giggled. "I don't care about all that and you know this. What do you want me to do to Mr. Giri?"

"Say his name and tell him to go deeper!" Anil's strokes strengthened as his hands roved over Katrina's breasts and under her nightie; fondling her hard nipples. His left hand caressed to her sides, her back, her butt and thighs. "Oh, beautiful, Katrina. Your skin's so soft and smooth. Your curves are amazing. It's so wonderful to fuck you tonight." Anil acted as Giri.

"Hmm. Keep stroking, big G."

"You're my first and I love it. Am I doing OK?" Anil was displaying signs of almost unloading.

"You're doing fine, baby!"

"Oh, god, it feels so good. Oh, darling, is it good—"

Before Katrina answered, Anil exploded. His spasms were strong as he grunted through them with his torso tightening. Katrina never felt him so intense and pleasured before.

When her husband finished ejaculating, Katrina asked, "That was kind of weird. What made you like this fantasy? I never seen you cum like that before?"

Anil rolled over breathing heavily as Katrina jerked his dick and played with the jizz. "It's a pleasure to know your woman is desired by others. It really turns me on."

"Ok, but—" Katrina grabbed a towel to wipe her privates and went to wipe Anil's. "Wow! You came so much, baby!"

This was the couple's first episode of fantasizing. Later that day, Katrina went online while her husband was at work to read about fantasizing. She discovered there's a primitive natural tendency for men to compete and found also that men actually ejaculate more and have stronger orgasms when there was competition whether past or present. She clicked on a website called 'Sperm Wars' which went into more details but still wasn't turned on by its subject.

Katrina remembered the guy Giri left the city to work with the Central Government. With that, his ghost faded from her memory a long time ago.

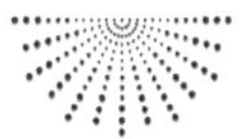

# CHAPTER ONE

That Giri fantasy was a thing of the past until one hot summer day, when Indian-English couple, David and Anita their friends, had a power outage and spent the night.

Late in the evening, Anil went into the shared bathroom adjoining where the visitors were sleeping. He didn't expect nothing unusual but he heard something.

There was panting, moans and groans by both for a few minutes. Then a short break and then more mumbled words mixed with sounds of pleasure and then the unmistakable, almost unrestrained voicing of a climax. Anil's dick was in his hand and he was stroking himself through his pyjamas when he realized someone might want to use the bathroom and slipped out beforehand.

When he got back to the bedroom, he found Katrina in bed with their iPad.

"Where were you?" She saw Anil's hand near his dick. "What are you doing in the bathroom?"

"Oh, my god. You should've heard them. They were fucking like animals."

"Oh my god! You were spying on them?"

"No. I was in the bathroom and heard the sounds. It was mind blowing!"

"Baby, you don't feel ashamed jerking off to others when you have me. I don't want to hear anymore of this nonsense!" Katrina went back to using her iPad.

"Oh please, honey. Help me. I am so turned on."

Katrina looked her husband, put the tablet aside and saw his face. Anil was an excited wreck. After a brief thought, she called him over and sat behind him to give him a hand job. It was something she was good at, always feeling she was in control. The way Anil ejaculated as she stroked him and she adored the stringy cum flying out in jerks. Katrina knew Anil's body well and could read his impending climax.

Katrina started working on him and then stopped briefly to pull up her nighty and pull down her panties. She knew Anil liked looking at privates as it made his love stick harder. Katrina's redden, smooth thighs and flat stomach and the hairy young pussy would turn the entire country on.

"Ooh, I want to fuck!"

"But I'm not ready!" She put her arm around Anil inviting him to suck her breasts. He loved doing that.

"Oh, my god those two are so sexy. They were really having hot sex. You should've heard them."

"Anil! I am not interested in that freaky stuff and I wish you weren't too!"

Anil was bringing his fantasy back. "Can we both pretend to be them just tonight? It'll be fun." He went back to sucking Katrina's breasts. His hands went downwards rubbing Katrina's clit causing her to moan. "Come on, baby. Let's go to another world."

"No! This is our world. Come and make love to me now. Just you and me."

Anil moved over and Katrina took his love stick and rubbed it on herself. Anil slipped in and they were in rhythmic sync and immersed in joy.

"Ah! It's so good. It feels so good. Do you wish

David could do this to you? Oh, I wish I was fucking Anita!"

She scrunched but said nothing. Anil continued but felt like he was fucking a statue. He climaxed after a few minutes and then rolled over. Meanwhile, Katrina remained silent and cold.

Anil didn't try to making peace and knew there was no point when Katrina was in that mood. He turned away and slipped into sleep. Katrina laid back thinking Anil must stop this foolish behavior or it would destroy their marriage.

# CHAPTER TWO

Though that incident caused a dent in Anil and Katrina's relationship for a while, things eventually returned to normal.

Katrina got a mammogram and ultrasound screening as it was discovered that her aunt was in the early stages of breast cancer. During Katrina's most recent visit, the radiologist recommended that she be checked out by a specialist as there was a lesion found but not life-threatening. As Katrina panicked, she was informed that she and her husband's close friend, Dr. David Vijayan, was there at the office and would be examining her right away.

Katrina thought of calling Anil first but decided against it since she knew David already.

David walked in giving Katrina smiling.

"Didn't expect to see you here. How are you feeling?"

"I'm okay. Just this—"

"Don't worry! We will have you out of here in no time." David went on to explain what the radiologist found and steps on further action.

As David walked away, a nurse prepared her. Katrina was wearing only the hospital gown with no bra on. She was told to take the gown off and lie down. David came back in again and Katrina nodded when he asked her if he could examine her breasts.

Over the next several minutes, David's fingers were on every inch of her breasts. He was so gentle and soothing in his words making Katrina feel reassured and comfortable. She was so relaxed that her nipples hardened. As David's hand brushed over her areolas, Katrina struggled knowing that his actions were getting her wet and felt so ashamed of herself.

Finally, the examination came to an end and Katrina was wondering if that was what she wanted or not. She pulled the sheet over herself quickly and clumsily the back of her hand hit David's privates.

"Oh gosh," she thought. What is happening?

Dr. David told her she would be OK and that she should have required to have a regular check-up and a needle biopsy soon.

* * *

On her drive home, Katrina thought about that night when Anil spied on David and Anita. Somehow that scene played over and over in her head and Katrina wondered why. Yet, she was having these sensual thoughts about the doctor earlier. Feelings of guilt gripped her and she felt so bad. After all, the right things taught to Katrina when growing up and never ever being unfaithful to her husband even in thought, this was the first time she had these weird feelings. She tried her best to push her thoughts aside but the memory of David's gentle fingers on her breasts felt so good.

So good that Katrina put her left hand up her skirt and touched her vagina feeling some wetness there! "Oh, my god," she thought.

Katrina reached home and waited for Anil to come to make rough and passionate love to her. She wanted his hard dick to ravage her pussy in every way possible to cleanse her of those naughty thoughts. Anil had to stop by his parents' home where he's gone to visit that afternoon.

As Katrina showered, cooked dinner, set the table and brought out a bottle of wine, she couldn't help but feel David's fingers brush past her nipples with that maddening amount of anticipation.

She sighed and then heard the garage door opening as she battled within herself if she should tell her husband. Katrina quickly decided she won't be telling him everything. He hadn't even remembered that his wife was going for her mammogram and Katrina forgot to call him as she usually did. Things were going in the wrong direction.

* * *

After their child, Anil, Jr. was showered, fed and put to bed, the couple had dinner and turned off the lights. Katrina showed as unusual amount of enthusiasm and Anil played along. It was when they reached their favourite position in lovemaking that Katrina brought the topic of her mammogram.

Anil was right at the point of having his pyjamas pulled down and Katrina had her fingers curled around his love stick stroking him gently. His fingers were inside her wet vagina and he was sucking her breast at the same time.

"I had my mammogram today and—"

"Oh yeah. It totally slipped my mind. How did it go?" He stopped to look at Katrina. "Everything alright?"

"Yes, hubby. Thank God everything is okay. Please don't stop doing what you were doing!"

They were quickly into sexual union once again. Somehow this night was different. Katrina thrashed about much more opening herself wider. She moaned louder especially as Anil stroked when both her legs were in the air. She clawed his back that almost broke skin when he was on top. Katrina's wet pussy made the most vulgar slurping sounds as Anil pounded. Katrina kept panting and whispering: "Oh my god!" Her last count was at three; the number of times Katrina came.

Minutes later, Anil held his breath as he strained to say: "I'm cumming!" Katrina slipped her hand down and held his wet dick giving it some adjuvant strokes to drain Anil fully. Her other hand went down to his butt muscles and then down to stroke Anil's balls.

He came every tiny bit into her and Katrina didn't know why she had a peculiar habit of counting his ejaculatory strokes. She counted eighteen. It was normally nine to eleven!

Even more fascinating is that during their love-making session, she thought again of David; when Anil fondled, and sucked her breasts; when his fingers were on her clit and inside her pussy and even when he climaxed.

Somehow, Katrina was now sucked into fantasy mode and it was hypocritical of her.

# CHAPTER THREE

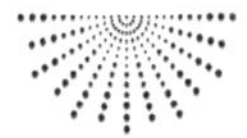

A few weeks later, one morning as Anil and Katrina were getting set for work when Anil complained of some stomach trouble. He sat for a while on the couch; his hands on his knees, and began sweating profusely. Katrina called the doctor and her mother-in-law. Just as the ambulance arrived, Anil collapsed.

They made it to the hospital in time and Anil was taken directly to the emergency room. The paramedics then escorted Katrina and Anil's mother out as they began resuscitation and after some initial sinister signs, they came out and told the two they were successful in reviving Anil. The lead doctor had said Anil had had a heart attack, which what they called a myocardial infarction.

The medical staff was ordered to swiftly shift him to a local hospital while he was still in critical condition.

* * *

Just days ago before Anil's heart attack, their English doctor friends, David and Anita, had moved apart and Anita moved out with their son. At the bedside with her husband still unconscious, David interjected at times mentioning his ordeal with Katrina. When he dropped her at home late that evening, he revealed even more. Katrina opened up speaking about her husband's many flings before their marriage.

Reflecting on her frank discussions with David over the last few days, Katrina felt streaks of guilt. However, as a result of the prolonged discussions, Katrina and David became very close. Awaiting the bleak outcome of her husband, Katrina began feeling strong emotions of attachment to David which she couldn't explain why.

After three days of Anil being in the hospital, the

head cardiologist called Katrina on the drive home revealing that the 'Copeptin Test' had indicated that her husband will pass away within days possibly weeks. She was sitting in David's car and his hands covered hers. For the first time, he touched her and Katrina curled her fingers to reciprocate. Suddenly, she felt guarded.

As Katrina was on the phone, David observed Katrina's movements in whatever she was wearing seeing she was an absolute beauty. His wife, Anita was big, curvy and sexy in a slutty way, Katrina was a pure unspoilt beauty. Her curves were subtle yet ample and she always carried an aura of innocence and a mantle of Hindu conservatism. Deep inside, David had always envied Anil's prized possession.

Katrina spent time with David during the days with her son, Anil, Jr. depending on the Englishman for emotional support After nineteen heart wrenching days, Katrina was informed that Anil had passed away due to a coronary artery that was blocked.

Katrina felt numb, stunned, and shocked. There was one single pillar to lean and that was David.

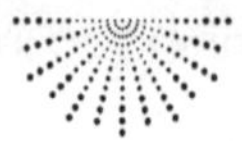

# CHAPTER FOUR

When Anil passed and the rites were over, Katrina and David had a heart-to-heart chat. They discussed their relationship if it could be possible. Love hadn't entered the scene yet and they dwelt on what kind of an impression they were creating within the conservative society they were living in. There would be rumoring which worried Katrina. Yet, they met everyday seeing they had to do it rather surreptitiously. Indian societal norms were judgemental!

It was also inevitable that they would begin to get intimate. David lived alone while Katrina had her son. She declined his invitations to his home for dinner as she was not sure of what she wanted in a new relationship.

Finally, one evening, Katrina has went to David's home and they were in his living room kissing passionately. Their bodies were pressed against each other; David's hands were squeezing her breasts. Katrina smiled licking her lips as she remembered the first time he had touched her that day in the doctor's office. They had discussed that and even if Katrina wouldn't initiate it, she wanted David to take her top and bra off to feel his fingers run across her.

David gestured towards his bedroom and soon enough, they were in bed together. Her nakedness occurred quite naturally sans shyness but punctuated with tiny bits of guilt. No other man other than her deceased husband had seen her naked. Katrina's desire to please, however, was unashamedly displayed in her eyes. David kindled even more as his eyes feasted on Katrina's body. He uttered words of praise of every single feminine attribute of hers, before his gentle fingers trailed his eyes. Inevitably, his lips followed leaving Katrina a quivering mess.

"Oh, you make me feel so good. I haven't felt like this in a long time. But... but we can't. We can't...fuck!"

"Why not?"

"I— I'm just not ready to go there. It's not you. I want you but, please…" Katrina held David's face in her palms and kissed him. "You don't understand, do you?"

"Nope!"

When she was speechless, David went back to her breasts kissing them each and playing with her perky light brown nipples. His hands roamed Katrina's body, familiarizing himself with those lovely curves, crevices and valleys. When David slipped down to her pussy, she groaned and then he moved down into her clit to see how wet she was. He mumbled and quickly brought his face down between her thighs tasting her saltiness and smelling her feminine fragrance which was magnetic. He licked before dwelling with the tip of his tongue on her swollen clit. Katrina arched her back and almost asked him to fuck her.

But she resisted that temptation and took another route. She looked down seeing his hard dick. She reached down and held it. Looking at it closely, Katrina pushed aside thoughts of comparisons. She started jerking David, slowly initially, then went faster and faster.

He let go of her and laid flat to enjoy her ministrations as Katrina went on switching hands to give his love stick uninterrupted strokes. She thought of sucking it and decided against it. David knew he was going to come as he groped around for some tissue. Katrina brought her free hand to gently caress his scrotum as they watched the cum spurt nearly hitting Katrina in the face. David panted his way through with grunts and moans.

"Oh god, Katrina! That was—"

"There's so much more we can have."

Katrina actually couldn't believe she was with a married man; her husband's good friend just 55 days after his death and had broken her traditional moral barriers.

There were a few of these episodes and all at David's place. She wanted them to go out and be normal but again there was that societal stigma. So, they were cooped up behind closed doors and since Katrina wasn't ready to have sex, she ended up giving David hand jobs. She saw David as a pretty decent guy.

Then one day it happened and it panned out beautifully. They had cooked up a good story among friends who might miss them and executed a plan to visit a resort. David left a day early on business and picked Katrina up in the city outskirts. They checked into a resort called 'The Lark's Louvre' tucked away in the curve of a valley and below the peaks of mountains. Their room on the top floor had tinted glass towards the west. Katrina was shocked to see that even the bathroom had a window covering the whole wall in direction of the valley.

"Wow!" Katrina gasped. "How can you shower when the whole valley is looking at you?"

"That's the point, my lady. The whole world wants to see you."

"Crazy. Stop being naughty, David."

Soon, they began showering together as nature looked on. In the dusk, their reflections were captured on the glass and Katrina thought they looked amazing. David looked at Katrina's beautiful figure glistening in soapy wetness; her hair plastered to her head and neck. He stood behind her and massaging her neck, then her breasts, tickling her nipples, going up to her lovely face and then moving down to her stomach to her vaginal area. Katrina moaned as David moved down her thighs causing Katrina to open herself to go further.

She looked through the glass at the hutments

now with flickering lights down below. "Someone may be looking with binoculars, you know."

"Those folks are not those types. I didn't tell you. This is a one-way glass!"

Katrina looked back looking naughty. "That might be a disappointment to you, huh?"

"A bit, I guess. I'd want the people to watch me with you."

They embraced as the warm flow from the shower got rid of the suds. Their hands moved over each other, scrubbing, caressing and fondling. When they toweled afterward, David posed the inevitable.

"I want to make love to you today, Katrina."

A nod dressed with a shyness was her answer. Then Katrina did what she always did. Standing in the shower stall, she grabbed David's love stick, drew back the skin, went on tip toeing and rubbed her moistness with the tip.

"Come, darling." She whispered. "You have waited enough. Make love to me! Now!"

"Say it raw, baby. Say 'fuck me'"

"OK... Fuck me and fuck me good!" David was surprised to hear Katrina talk dirty for the first time.

They hurried back to bed with the wetness in Katrina's hair matching that between her thighs. She rubbed David's dick against her slit several times and going far up to rub her clit to a good measure. The desire pounding in her ears as she took him in for the first time. Months of no sex did not have the resistance she feared. David entered in and the awesome rhythm he developed had Katrina moaning; she hoisted her lower limbs up and around his hard chest. David felt her softness and her yielding flesh giving the couple much excitement.

Almost simultaneously, they remembered they had no protection. A quick unwanted interruption but it didn't matter. They resumed as if nothing happened and soon David climaxed causing Katrina to respond with hefty thrusts upwards.

When their moans ended along with with their passion they laid side by side.

"Are we OK? I mean—"

"Of course, sweetheart. Was it good?"

"It was wonderful. And for you?" Katrina rubbed David's face.

"It was great. You are such a giving person. You gave yourself fully."

"You filled me, honey. And I don't mean physically either." Katrina carefully censored her words. "I want to tell you something."

David's ears perked. "Ok, I'm all ears."

"Hmm...Do you remember when you and Anita stayed with us that evening when you had the power outage?"

"Of course, I do. Why?"

"No. It's just that... just that Anil heard you guys fucking in that room. Sorry for my blatant expression. He was so excited!"

"Wow!" David had an interesting expression on his face.

"I know some guys like to be voyeurs. I apologize on behalf of my late husband."

"No, not that! Do you remember Anita and you were at the salon earlier that day?"

"Yeah. What about it?"

"Anita told me she saw your body and—"

"I was in my undies!"

"Whatever she said, she saw you and was so impressed. She kept talking about your shape and skin. It was as if she was turned on by you."

Katrina giggled. "Girls are like that sometimes. Almost bisexual."

"Did you even want to do that it to another woman?"

"Never!" Katrina laughed.

"Our sex that night was a fantasy of you in our bed and it was so exciting. Anita kept saying that you were so smooth and sexy and that I would love to have you. Anita is a hairy everywhere. Who would've thought that we'd be like this?"

"Didn't know that. Do you miss her?"

"No, not at all. Why now when I have the best in the world. Even Anita thought so." David turned towards her and ran a gentle finger tip over Katrina's nipples. "You are so beautiful."

"But what will happen to us then? How can we go on like this in secret?"

"I don't know." David then changed subjects. "Back to that night, I am shocked that both of us were thinking of each other. My god, were you thinking of me?"

"Not really. Anil was thinking of us both being you both. So, I don't know." Katrina laughed. "I'm not into the fantasy thing. Anil kept telling me that it's only play. I went with him as it made him happy."

"Did he fantasize a lot?"

"There was a guy named Giri, who used to hit on me a lot. Anil used to ask me to think that it was him having sex with me a few times. That's it."

"Oh! Tell me about Giri. How did that work? I mean imagining him being with you?"

"I don't know. I don't get turned on like that."

"Ok, so what turns you on? Fantasy wise? Tell me your best fantasy."

"Hmm. It's long. Will you be patient?"

"Yes, please go ahead." David's fingers slipped down over her stomach and onto her soft private area.

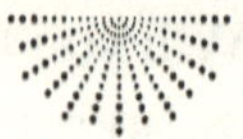

"The mood and ambience is everything for me. I would love for it to be a cool day in a beautiful place surrounded by nature. I guess like this place. The guy should be very caring, loving and help me cook an amazing dinner. I would bring out the best bottle of red wine and he would pop the cork. We would sit down in our dining room overlooking the sunset over a fountain that sprays misty haziness around. We will have some amazing Hindi music. Ah! Oh! You are distracting me." Katrina reacted with a whisper to David's finger that had slipped into her pussy. She closed her eyes and continued.

"We eat our dinner slowly and his gaze is on me the whole time. I'll return the compliment with a smile and a seductive look of invitation. The man then hovers over my neck and shamelessly stares at my breasts. I shift uncomfortably and adjust my top in false modesty to hide my cleavage. He says, "I'm beautiful." This is our first time and he's eager. I am too but less obvious. The man stands up and walks up to my side and as we finish eating and he slowly undresses me while I help him. I stand naked next to the dining table at the gathering of orange dusk. Hotness is what I feel and I need him to devour me and he surely does; right against the wall and then up on the kitchen counter and then against the glass door. I beg for him to take me inside to enjoy his dinner in quiet darkness. The man hesitates but complies."

Katrina didn't miss the fact that she was fantasizing.

She looked at him and slid her own hand along his side and found his penis lying semi turgid on his thigh. "Nice." He said, in simple appreciation. She felt him going hard and big in her fingers and she smiled.

"Do you want to make love again?"

"What do you think?"

David was onto her in a jiffy. Katrina's pussy was so wet and easy to enter. David surely wanted to taste her goodness once more. Katrina didn't even have a second to hold him and play with herself as she normally would. David came quickly and she responded with some mock jerks to make him happy.

They soon fell asleep.

That was the beginning of a very intimate, secret relationship. The couple enjoyed each other's company and had sex on many occasions. No one really knew what was going on though both were often suspected by those in their circles.

But that didn't last long.

David had applied for a position as a surgeon in Oman and months later was contacted. The offer was extremely lucrative and difficult to refuse.

David and Katrina had lengthy talks on how they could go on. Katrina did not want to leave India and David didn't want to pass up the offer on the table. He also considered a change of scene after the finalization of his divorce.

Ultimately, they agreed it was best to part ways and over the first year or so, they kept in touch.

David was the more enthusiastic as physical love was what he missed most. Katrina, on the other hand, missed his company, support and friendship and longed for those more spiritual facets. She spent time focusing on her widowed life and profession. All she wanted for herself and her son was to be comfortable in life.

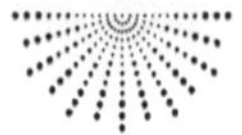

It was then that Giri came back into Katrina's world. He was still single but had risen up the ranks in the Central Government. He travelled extensively within India and abroad and therefore it was a bit odd that he hadn't married yet. People rumored that he was gay but he was not. He reasoned that his heart broke when Katrina and Anil had married. Honestly, she already knew this. Then, it happened that Katrina ran into him at a restaurant one late afternoon after work.

"Why didn't you get married?" Katrina started the conversation with the obvious.

"Oh, you didn't think I tried?" Giri described his attempts in detail; profile on Tinder and Shaadi, his exploits with suitors that didn't match, his aunt's inconsistent efforts, and etc.

As he was getting a bit emotional, Katrina got a hint of his eyes welling up which caused her to feel sorry for him.

"Don't worry, Giri. It's not too late. You're a great guy and there are girls out there. I will look around for you."

"But why—why can't you, say yes?" Girl moaned. "You're single and so am I. What's the problem?"

"I don't see you like that. Besides I'm older than you. I don't think I have what you are looking for."

"I am looking for a woman, for god's sake!" Giri looked at Katrina for a positive reaction and then a sudden wave of regret and pride came over him. "OK. Fine. I'm not going to beg."

They sat silently as the orange sunset was swallowed by the dusk descending slowly with symbolic gloom for Giri. It happened to also cloud Katrina's judgement.

"I'm leaving on Tuesday. Can I see you on Sunday? For lunch, maybe?" He looked into her eyes and detected a softening within.

"OK." Katrina smiled with very little hesitation. "Where?"

"I'll pick you up. We'll decide afterward."

* * *

When Sunday arrived, Giri rang Katrina to tell her he would like them to go to the Elite Club and have swim before lunch. Katrina was hesitant but agreed. She put on her light-brown swimsuit that matched her skin colour and she looked maddeningly sexy in it.

They chatted by the poolside and then as they slipped into the shallow end. "What have you been doing with yourself, Katrina? I mean. your private life. Did you not see anyone? I can't believe every man has left you alone in this big city."

"Well, Giri, I've had more attention than I expected but there wasn't a good fit. Those that I liked weren't free and those that liked me weren't for me." She didn't want to mention David because she knew Giri knew him.

"What about David, the doctor? There was some chatter about him messing around with his patients after his divorce. Wasn't you one of them?" Giri giggled.

"What?" Katrina feigned in anger. "He was a close friend to both Anil and me. I personally know people who were talking at the time but I wasn't into him like that."

Giri had a knowing smile and he wasn't buying that story. "I see," muttered Giri without discussing more.

Meanwhile, Katrina tried her best to sway off her inner-tinglings as those hot encounters with David popped up in her mind.

Then, a bit of pity for Giri dawned on Katrina. From her husband, David and from reading about men, she knew how he felt. There was a desire to know more about him but what business is it of hers?

"What are you thinking, Katrina?"

"I'm wondering how you are managing being alone."

"Why? Do I look like I can't manage?"

"No, no! Not that. Everyone needs a partner, you know."

"I could ask you the same!"

"True." She thought. "Women are different. They can get involved in stuff and still exchange those emotions for something else. Men can't."

"Oh, interesting." David couldn't hide the fact that he craved to be with a woman, feel her softness and make love to her whenever he please. He prided himself in not going after prostitutes. That wasn't easy as they were all around in the big city. But he still longed for Katrina. She was so beautiful even after all those years; looking so young, while that innocent pretty face. Her figure and complexion turned heads everywhere.

*She was also single, damn it!*

Giri was excited and couldn't keep himself from looking at her body. He kept imaging the heavenly flesh beneath. Her breasts with her stiffened nipples were pushing against the wet fabric. Her shapely butt that he once visually devoured in tight jeans on a holiday a decade earlier and then the lovely triangle where her thighs met; he kept fantasizing about the most.

Katrina, like most women would, noticed his eyes on her. She caught him glancing at her boobs on more than one occasion as she surfaced after swimming. She caught a glimpse of him checking out her thighs and even staring at her vaginal area. Without a doubt when Giri was behind her, he was surveying her derriere. She felt odd, on several occasions, she had to adjust her swimsuit, preventing it from creeping into crevices that might expose her more than she wanted. Yet, she also felt sexy, good and thought those sensations were coming to her after a long while.

After the swim, Katrina went into a cubicle and Giri slipped into the opposite. He dropped swiftly to the wet floor a bit away from the door and saw Katrina's feet. She stood moved around, perhaps toweling herself and then as her weight shifted from one foot the other he saw her swimsuit being pulled down. She picked it up and as Giri heard his poor heart pound, he wished those walls and doors would disappear for a few seconds so that his eyes might feast on what he desired most, just once in his long-frustrated life!

"Oh, god," Giri thought what a bit of torture as Katrina still stood there naked behind that door, drying herself. Then, he saw her hands bringing down a pair of panties to her lovely ankles and gently she stepped into them. Giri devoured every micro movement with astute clinical precision. Next, Katrina pulled her jeans up and within a minute, the door opened and she stepped out. The erection he had was unfulfilled.

Giri quickly changed and somehow managed to put up a normal face over lunch and then they parted for the day.

# CHAPTER SEVEN

Giri was back in the city again after six weeks. But not before days and nights of fanaticising and browsing porn sites on the web and satisfying himself with all the myriad avenues available therein. He stayed in touch with Katrina regularly messaging and calling looking for another wonderful opportunity to meet her. She told him she was traveling to another state, six hours away for a conference on women's empowerment. Giri, lied to her saying he was invited for the same event. He extracted her travel plans through clever questioning and managed to book himself on the overnight train to the venue along with Katrina.

On the train journey after dinner they had

shared, Giri couldn't help pleading for Katrina's love and she told him why she couldn't accept.

In the dimmed lights, as other passengers turned in and both of them sitting huddled close together somehow the senses were more acute.

Giri told her that he never been with with another woman and didn't want to even think of another. He had many temptations to solicit prostitutes but hadn't. Yet, Giri told Katrina he'd been on porn sites since he was younger and pleasured himself in watching.

"Why are you telling me all this? These are very personal things that I really don't want to know." Katrina looked away out into the moonlight as the train passed by village homes.

"I want you to know how much I love you, Katrina. I am crazy about you. Do you not see?"

"I understand, Giri. But this is not love. I'm sorry you are unhappy. If I have led you on, I apologize. That was not my intention."

"No, you never." Their shoulders and knees were touching and Giri stroked the back of Katrina's hand. "But you're so gorgeous, I can't help myself."

"Tell me something honestly, Giri." Katrina

looked into his eyes. "And don't be mad at me for asking. Is it—sex that you are missing or are you looking for real love?"

Giri pondered unexpectedly. "Both, I guess!" He shook his head still confused. "How can they be separated?" He added with pretended wisdom. "It is eating me alive inside, I must admit. I spend hours thinking of what's missing often comparing myself with others."

Katrina held onto his fingers that were on her and looked at him intently. "I don't know what to say. I'm confused and it will kill me to see you like this. We were childhood friends and grew up together." Katrina then put her arms around Giri and in the dimness of the corner they were in, she kissed him on the cheek. "Now let's get some sleep. We have a busy day ahead."

With his Giri's mind reeling with the last few minutes of the conversation, he rolled back and forth not able to sleep. *Why did he not kiss her back? Why couldn't he hug her?* He was paralyzed blaming himself for lacking initiative with women in general.

Then as Giri relaxed, he had a short dream in which Katrina rejected his advances. He was glad when he woke up.

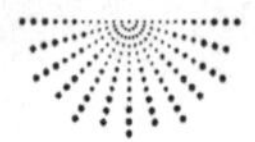

# CHAPTER EIGHT

Giri hoped he could spend more time with Katrina during the three-day meet but that was not decreed. On the first day after the session, she met up with a school friend, had dinner and spent a good part of the night with her. On the second evening, she had a dinner meeting with a group of activists that she had worked with. Giri became frustrated going into the last day seeing whatever momentum he had built on the train journey was not bearing fruit.

The third day's session rolled along aimlessly and as expected Giri had no contact with Katrina. He hoped in the evening he could finally spend some quality time with her. He even imagined he could lure her to his room and then who knows what will happen?

His heart then thudded when Katrina told him she was going out with some other friends and may even stay overnight.

And as known, Giri was disgusted!

He was convinced he was a failure if he couldn't attract a single widowed woman to even spend an evening with him, let alone a lifetime!

In a maddening moment, Giri picked up the phone and dialed Katrina's room.

"What the hell? I'm dying to be with you and you're simply avoiding me with a million and one excuses. It's either this person or that. Who are these fucking people anyway? Why are they so fucking important?"

"Calm down, Giri. Oh, my gosh! I have never heard you so angry. Don't be upset. My friend, Mallika needs to go back to Mumbai because her father had a heart attack. Fortunately, the evening program has been canceled."

"Oh!" Giri thought. "I hope he's OK." Giri didn't mean one bit of it. He mentally thanked the old man who gave him a chance.

"I hope so too. You know what? Why don't you come over to my room and we'll have dinner here? Is that OK with you?"

"Ok, of course. "I'll be there in a few minutes."

Within two minutes, Giri was at Katrina's door. He had changed; wearing a knock-off Supreme tee and shorts. Katrina was quick to comment.

"Oh, you've changed already. I've been busy on the phone," Katrina said gesturing for Giri to sit. "Take a look at the menu. I'll be back. I need to shower."

Giri's heart skipped a beat. "Goodness me," he thought. He was going to sit there when this gorgeous woman was going to shower? He should sit there jerking off. He nodded as Katrina looked back at him as she walked into the bathroom.

All kinds of erotic thoughts flashed through Giri's mind as he heard the water run. His eyes fell on a suitcase on the bed, unzipped with clothes coming out. He gingerly opened the suitcase seeing stuff just dumped in. He took out a pair of Katrina's pants and in a moment of depraved fetish, he smelt the crotch. Nothing except faint perfume. Giri looked around frantically for something more intimate. He found what he was looking for; a pair of lacy silk panties! He kissed, sniffed and hugged it. He sniffed over the crotch again. Was there a hint of Katrina's lingering exotic feminineness? Giri put everything back carefully. He imagined every inch of Katrina's naked body as possible realizing he had an erection.

Inside, in the shower, Katrina tried gathering her thoughts. This guy was going mad about her and she knew she was crazy to call him to her room for dinner. "Am I asking for it?" she thought. Of the many men after Anil and David who tried hitting on to her, Giri was the only one she had begun to consider at least for the moment. It's been a while since Katrina was with a man.

Katrina ran her hands over her breasts as the drops of water stiffened her light brown nipples. She ran her fingers down her pubic area and then down to the vertical slit that had not been permeated since David. Two men in Katrina's life had given her so much carnal pleasure and she had returned the favor. Katrina began imagining her stroking her slit with Giri's love stick inside.

"Oh, my goodness! What a moral wreck I have become with all the fantasizing and imagery?" pondered Katrina. After a minute of fantasizing, she pushed all those thoughts aside, ended her shower and toweled.

The bathroom door opened causing Giri's heart to gallop. Katrina stepped out in an orange tank top with black buttons and black blazer. Giri thought Katrina would be wearing her nighties but it was only in his imagination.

"What do you like to order?"

Giri opened the menu on the coffee table and read out the first thing he saw. "Tandoori and Naan. What about you?"

"Make that two."

"Anything to drink?"

"Ah! A Bloody Mary for me."

"OK."

Katrina called room service and ordered, adding a Scotch for her.

"It felt nice showering. This place is so humid," said Katrina sitting on the bed next to the suitcase that Giri had opened.

"Why are you so dressed up? Looks like you're planning to go out."

"What? Would you like me to change into my nighties?" Katrina laughed.

"Yeah, why not?"

"OK!" Katrina pretended to reach for her buttons to take her top off and stopped. She giggled knowing that she was teasing.

"Oh, my god! Please!"

"Ha! Think I'm that easy? You'll have to earn it."

"I'll do anything. Tell me."

"What do you want, Giri? You just want me to change into my nightie?"

"No. I want to see your body!"

Katrina blushed. She was startled and even a bit upset. Lurking deep inside was also a feeling of being appreciated. "Gosh! You have the balls to say that!"

"Please, don't be angry, my lady Just imagine. I'm 40 and I have been lonely and I feel I will never find a good woman. I'm a virgin and have never been with a woman once!" Giri looked down burying his face in his hands.

Katrina remained silent and before she had a chance to consider, room service had arrived. They switched to talking about the conference and speakers as they sipped their drinks and ate. Giri ordered another Scotch while Katrina declined. Unnoticed by Giri, Katrina released her large, black top button and took a quick glance in the mirror seeing her cleavage was on display.

When Giri downed his second drink, he began staring at Katrina's breasts. Katrina tried pulling up her top in pseudo-modesty but not before Giri feasted on her curves and boobs that poured over especially when she bent forward serving food or picking up something from the tray.

Then the loss of inhibitions provoked by arousal and alcohol took hold of Giri causing him to blurt: "Why don't you change into something sexy?"

"Oh, my god! You are losing control over yourself." Yet, Katrina beamed feeling a bit tipsy too. She was liking the attention Giri was giving her body. "Are you serious?"

"Of course. Come on."

"Take it easy, OK." She got up to rummage through her case and took out a garment that Giri thought was flimsy enough. Katrina turned to go into the bathroom.

"Wait. Change here."

Katrina stopped, tuned back with her hands on her hips. "What the heck?"

She walked back slowly as Giri's heart boomed. "OK." Katrina was ready to give in. "I will change here, but stay there, OK?" Then, Katrina flipped the lights off. Only a lamp and the bathroom lights were dimmed.

"We have a deal."

Katrina stood about ten feet away away,

dropping the nightie on the bed and slowly started unbuttoning her top. Her eyes were on him and Giri was mesmerized to stillness as he watched Katrina's beautiful breasts encased in a perfectly fitting bra emerge. He squinted and stared to grab his love stick to accommodate the dimness. Katrina's top was open but still on her shoulders. She parted the front to give Giri a good view and then suddenly, she quickly grabbed her nightie and slipped it over her head.

"No! No! No!" Giri shook his head. "Take the bra and blazers off."

"Have you gone mad? No one has seen me like since my husband."

"Oh, you're so stubborn. At least take your blazers off." His hand grabbed onto his crotch even harder and Katrina noticed. She knew he was turned on.

"OK." Katrina cleverly undid the button and pulled her pants down without revealing anything other than her legs from knee downwards. Then she sat. "Now what?" she now regretted what she asked.

"Oh, you want to do something else?" Giri giggled naughtily.

Katrina ignored his dry humor.

"You looked nice in the swimming pool the other day."

"I know you were looking too much."

"Oh, you noticed?"

"Women see stuff like that. They have a sixth sense."

"Hmm, then tell me where I was looking."

"Where men usually look."

"Where is that?"

"Do I have to tell you where you were looking? You know." Katrina giggled. "My chest a lot of times."

"Oh, did I? You do have some pretty boobs, Katrina. Do you mind showing them to me?"

"Gosh, you are really a freak!"

Giri wasn't sure if Katrina was joking or serious. "Have you gone mad or are you drunk?"

"I am crazy for you and not so drunk. Just having a good buzz. Come on, baby. Show me!"

Katrina was jolted by him saying the word 'baby'. She had to admit that after so long she was sort of enjoying a man's advances.

However, she said: "No!"

"Aw, what a spoiled sport!"

"I think it's time for us to say goodnight."

Katrina didn't believe she meant that and Giri caught her drift.

"If I go now, you'll regret it." He leered. "Listen, Katrina. You're such a beautiful woman and are still young. Do you think you can survive being alone?"

"I don't miss a man, Giri. Understand that a woman's brain works differently." She looked away as she spoke: "And I know how a man's works especially his penis."

"I guess you know everything about us. I mean no harm. I just want to see a woman who I've wanted since childhood and if you don't fulfill my desire, who will?"

There was no answer from Katrina. She thought about what Giri said looking at him. Giri was seeing her defenses drop. "What do you want to see? And what will you do afterward?"

His face brightened. "I want to see you nude. That's all. I won't touch you."

"You want to see everything? That's too much!"

"OK. Just show me your breasts."

Katrina looked at him without any perceivable emotion. Then, she stood up and without saying a word, walked into the bathroom.

Was she going to come out nude?

Katrina emerged just as she was all clothed.

"What the—" Giri began but stopped as he saw Katrina's naughty smile.

She walked straight up to him, stood about five feet away and pulled her nightie neck down to bring out her beautiful pair of breasts. She'd gone to the bathroom to shed her bra.

Giri simply stared at nature's wonderful creation. The perfect shape was enhanced with a lift provided by the neck of her garment supporting below. Her areolas and nipples were light brown, only a shade or two darker than the rest of her smooth skin. The nipples were hardened and erect in the titillating atmosphere. Katrina knew the effect she was having on Giri and also within herself.

"OK?" Katrina shrugged and popped her boobs back into her nightie.

"No! Please, I want to see more." Giri sounded like a juvenile.

"What more can you see by seeing it longer?" She brought her boobs out again, one by one.

Giri leaned forward to get a closer look and he popped the question.

"Can I—"

"No! No touching!"

"No, no. I want to—?" His hands were inching towards his crotch and Katrina knew what he was implying.

"Oh! My god! No! That's so disgusting! I can't believe we are doing this."

"Please!"

Katrina pondered. "OK, get behind that sofa and do what you want. I don't want to see you.."

Giri moved behind the chair, pulled a stool behind it, sat down and lowered his shorts bringing his erect penis out.

Katrina avoided looking and felt awkward standing there feeling like some cheap stripper. "Do it quickly. I don't want to stay like this for long."

Giri began stroking slowly and then quicken staring at Katrina's beautiful breast. "Can you not take off your nightie completely? Please?"

Katrina glanced at him making sure she didn't look downwards. She saw the raw desire and beastly lust in his eyes and the straining muscles of his face as he clenched his teeth while stroking himself with moans. She knew Giri was like the rest who were animals feasting shamelessly on her nudity when her clothes came off. David and Anil had told her that every bit of her intimate parts was desirable. David had often praised her butt; its roundedness and curviness. Anil had done the same but was always fascinated by her vagina's scent. All Katrina's girlfriends had complimented on her sexy figure and many men stared at her on the streets. Now this guy, whom she knew for decades is asking to see the same.

Without saying a word, Katrina started taking off her nightie. In her panties alone, she turned away and very slowly she peeled her underwear, wriggling her hips.

Giri gasped, then groaned and hissed out the words: "My god!" He stroked vigorously as he saw the shapeliness of Katrina's bare ass, the deep crevice, the prominent fold below that accentuated her protrusions. The glowing smooth skin topped it all with exotic sexiness. The exposed feminine buttock of his beloved in all its glory hit him like a streak of lightning. All the butts he had seen on porn paled in comparison.

"OK, now what?"

"Can you turn around, please?"

Katrina didn't answer. Her brain was working fast and that was the last frontier because of her conviction that this was the point of no return. And she was not even sure what could happen.

Giri ripped off all his clothes and stood up. His

joints cracked to alert her and Katrina glanced over her shoulder and turned back quickly. "Oh, my gosh!" she muttered realizing he was nude holding his love stick.

Katrina froze as he walked up to her and shuddered as his left hand touched her shoulder and then almost coaxed her to turn. In a trance sans reasoning, she slowly submitted to the pressure of his hand facing him as their eyes met.

Katrina saw desire in his eyes and realized she had the beginnings of an urge coming on. In one gush, she felt moistness seep into her vaginal area. The next moment, Katrina put her arms around Giri's inexperienced self and brought his lips to hers. His hands grabbed her waist and then loosened in confused distraction as her sweet lips and tongue ignited his soul.

She felt his manhood pointing upwards pressed against her and she dared not look downward. She didn't want him to see her raw nakedness too quickly. They disengaged as his hands slipped down to her butt. Giri was surprisingly gentle for a novice.

"Oh, how smooth and soft you are!" Giri spluttered. "Oh, marry me!"

What a time to propose! Katrina almost laughed. His nimble fingers on her butt distracted her though. He was moving very slowly towards her crack and then moved down to even more sensitive areas.

They kissed again as Giri's hands parted Katrina's ample buttocks and the tip of his index finger felt the puckered skin of her butt's opening. It was erotic for him and it tickled Katrina's senses even more. She went deep into his mouth and Giri matched hers with his own thrashing.

They moaned out loud ignoring the possibility of being heard. His penis kept poking her stomach feeling the coarse fuzziness Katrina's pubic hair brush his thighs. They separated as Katrina wanted to caress his hairy chest; her fingers rode over a nipple and then his naval and was about to go lower but at the last second she backed off.

"Ooh, my darling. This is what I have been waiting for. Please, darling. Can I fuck you?"

She looked into his eyes. Her demeanor softened and her desire to please him now quite evident. "Don't ask," she whispered. "Just be relax and be yourself. It may happen."

He stepped back a bit and glanced downwards. Katrina's breasts were beautiful. Her nipples were hard and pointy. Whatever little sag she had was overwhelmed by volume. The core of her woman-hood was now on full display

Giri simply looked into her eyes and didn't even utter a word lowering himself slowly. Preparing for an extremely slow and deliberately stretched intro-duction to the world of sex. Katrina waited almost impatiently as he kissed her neck and breasts for what seemed like hours before he made progress.

Giri hesitated to go down but Katrina placed her hands on the sides of his head, then moved it down to her pubic area.

"Do you like what you see?" Katrina's voice was hoarse filled with arousal. "Look at me fully. This is what you wanted, right?"

"You're so beautiful, Katrina. I can't even believe this is happening." He got on his knees and slowly moved his head inwards. Her hands remained on his head guiding it.

Katrina continued to be marveled at the sheer beauty of her physique looking in the mirror at Giri on his knees before her.

"Hmm... Touch me gently, Giri. Gently!" Katri-na's request was almost a whisper. He turned his forefinger to face upwards and he made a soft swipe upwards on her moist pussy lips; his first ever touch of feminineness.

Giri looked at its slimy surface and realized what wetness truly meant. "Oh gosh!" he gasped. "Why are you so wet?" he said looking up for an answer and all he got was a smile.

As if encouraged and possessed with a force of lust all at once, Giri grabbed Katrina's buttocks with both hands and brought her pussy to his thirsty, virgin lips. He drank from her core as he imbued his senses with the glorious scent of womanhood. His lips lapped at the erotic saltiness of the centre of Katrina's being that was bridled unfairly and wastefully for so long.

Katrina began breathing heavily and shut her eyes in enjoyment while Giri deployed his tongue into her waiting cavity to touch, stroke and paint her insides with passionate ministrations of an anxiously-inspired debutant.

Katrina then gripped his head and moved her hands and fingers over his head and face and egged him on to higher planes of her own arousal. Her hips moved back and forward and left and right seeking unrealistic strata of gratification. Giri's fingers digging into her soft buttocks were almost forgotten. Katrina just let out one huge moan of satisfaction, oblivious to the decibels that rang through the room.

"Oh, Giri. You are doing good. Come here." She gestured for him to stand. Without looking down, she felt his throbbing love stick and caressed its smooth skin thumbing its tip. Her secret arousing techniques were coming back.

Giri arched back as he had his mouth open with no sound. The incredible feeling of a women's palm on him was almost shocking. His eyes were wide open in heightened arousal as Katrina continued to jerk. He quickly felt the imminent danger; his ejaculation coming.

He grabbed her hand suddenly that Katrina stiffened and looked down to see him. His dark cock with her stroking was a beautiful site.

"What happened? Did I hurt you?"

"No. The opposite. I almost came!"

"It's okay!" Katrina wrapped her arm around him. "You can come."

"But I want to—"

"Yes, I want that, too. We can do that later. Don't hold back now, darling. Just come for me." She continued jerking him so expertly yet gently until he exploded.

Giri grunted uncontrollably as he squirted up years of built-up desire onto Katrina's neck and breasts. Katrina stood letting Giri cum onto her furry pubes and even let his last mighty thrust near her lips.

Giri's cum was on her breasts and stomach while tiny beads tickled as they trickled down the insides of her thighs. She counted nine spasms! Giri's eyes were closed treasured in a starved man's brain forever. Katrina stroked him gently again once more before she let finally let go.

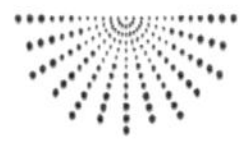

# CHAPTER NINE

Giri opened his eyes smiling wrapping one arm around Katrina while his fingers reached down for her pussy. He felt the wetness of its aura.

"Put your finger inside and feel me. See how you soaked me, Giri."

Giri gently entered and felt the insides for the first time. He knew he had to be gentle.

"Why did you deny me this? Why did you keep me waiting so long?

"Come!" Katrina whispered as she sat back on the bed and raised her hand beckoning. Her legs parted invitingly and she had the sexiest smile. "I will teach you everything—everything!"

Giri's momentary flaccid state gave way to another powerful erection. He dwelt for a moment on Katrina's privates admiring the shape of her shiny lower vagina lips and pubic hair. He glanced over those hips and thighs and devoured those breasts again.

"You are so lovely. Every inch of you." Giri leaned over Katrina pushing her back on the bed as she reached down to hold him in helping him enter her. "Wait a minute." He said as he raised up grabbing his pants on the ground. He took out a condom.

"You came prepared my boy?" Katrina was a bit annoyed.

"I always carry one just in case."

"Liar!"

"I swear it's true." He ripped off the foil, brought out the flimsy red thing and quickly put it on assuming his position above Katrina once more.

Then abruptly, Katria said: "Stop. Take that thing off. I'm on birth control. Let me feel you naked!"

"Wow!" was all Giri could manage to utter. He tore the condom off and lowered himself as Katrina held him. "Am I big enough for you?"

"There you go, you stupid men. Size is nothing.

At least for me." She drew him towards her cunt. "Let me tell you what most men don't know. They are unaware of the angle of entry. It's backwards and upwards as you enter when the woman lies flat." Katrina pulled him gently in and then Giri thrust himself deep into her. The feeling of being swallowed finally almost overtook him.

"How do you know this?"

"What?"

"That most men don't know that stuff."

"Oh, I have been with a few men. What did you think?"

"Really?"

"You jealous?"

"Maybe. But you never wanted me!"

"You, silly boy! Of course, I was only with Anil. Who do you think I am? Now hurry up and fuck me before I change my mind! Go in and out. These are the basics."

Giri slipped out and then tried to enter her again but was hitting something.

"A little lower. Giri adjusted. "Just a wee bit. Yeah, not too much. Now go in!"

He was not still making progress beyond the first inch.

"I told you to go slightly upwards, honey. Down and up, remember?"

Bullseye for the second try. Giri went deep and then his instincts grabbed hold. He went from slow to very fast in a few seconds, grunting panting and all.

"Hold on, Giri. The girl enjoys when your whole dick rubs her inside. That's the best for both partners. Just come out almost completely and then go in deep." When Giri improvised, Katrina added: "And slow is better in the beginning."

Giri's senses were all focused on himself but something told him to take care of Katrina's body so he moved his hands randomly over her. She, in turn, moved her fingertips to glide over his buttocks and stealthily moved between his thighs to touch his balls. She knew what that did to men. Giri responded with a groan.

"Do things to me, too." Katrina cooed. "Feel my breasts and kiss them." Her legs went up in the air and wrapped around Giri's butt.

He bent down to satisfy her moving his hips and syncing his lips to the rhythm. Katrina's soft fingers playing with his balls and then creeping down between them to hold his love stick was too much for him.

"Oh, Katrina—Ooh! I am going to cum." No sooner had Giri uttered those words and before Katrina could react, he ejaculated and moaned through his strokes. She jerked with him in union still not satisfied.

"Thank you very much!"

"Don't say that. It sounds like a favour. We were in it together." She spoke as she kept jerking his manhood. "You came so quickly for the second time. You need to hold on, you know. Girls need time."

"Oh, sorry."

"No, don't be sorry. Just make me come, not in this instance but before you."

"How? Please teach me."

"Sure, I will. Give me your hand." Giri did so. "Come look at me and see some more anatomy." Katrina giggled.

Giri turned and moved towards Katrina's sticky pussy. She took his index finger and placed it in.

"Turn the light on. It's too dark."

Katrina flipped the bed side switch revealing a gentle orange glow that lit her nakedness.

Katrina then parted her lips with two fingers to given him a good view and with his finger held in, she made those thin circles on the centre of her pussy. "You see these gentle, circular movements."

Giri began well but got a bit rough.

"Ouch! Gently."

"Sorry."

"Yeah, good. You are learning!" Katrina was quiet as Giri continued and reminded himself that he needed to be gentle. He quickened his pace when he saw her eyes shut and let her knees fall apart in enjoyment. Soon, there were soft moans that followed and deep breathing and then finally loud moans. Katrina's hands reached out. Holding his arms and then his chest, she reached between his legs. "Put this in me and suck my breast. Oh lord!" She was wriggling with arousal and fulfilment.

Katrina pushed his hand aside and started masturbating herself.

"Why? Am I not doing it right?"

"Just keep quiet and fuck me. Now! Get that thing inside me! Kiss me and hurry up!"

With her free hand, Katrina guided Giri in, not giving him a chance to employ his newly acquired skill. Her hips rose to meet him and then thrashed about as he began pumping her. Giri was fully hard again and found her moving frantically beneath him.

"Oh gosh! Do something. Kiss me. Grab my ass. Suck my nipples!" Giri was amazed at Katrina's appetite for hard, rough sex. He let his latent instincts drive his copulatory actions. "Oh, my god!" Katrina yelled a strained whisper and then clenched her teeth as her back arched and then she came.

Katrina's body convulsed as Giri felt the creaming of his penis by her vaginal muscles and huge grunts escaped her lips. Her waves of climax surfaced, broke free and eventually subsided. Katria remained still in bliss hardly breathing for a few minutes.

Katrina smiled. "That was heavenly." She kissed Giri's cheek. "You're right. Maybe we should've done this earlier." She now realized she was actually missing sex, not a man.

Giri laid back, feeling proud of himself. Was this really happening?

Meanwhile, Katrina went on mental journey wondering if she was doing the right thing. Oh boy, she enjoyed it.

Why was Katrina holding this back for so long? Giri was after her since day one but there were others who were simply waiting to get inside her panties. And she just turned them all away. Was Katrina hard to get? Of course. Was she just being a good friend to Giri or was it more than that?

"I love those breasts; the way the tips are just only a shade darker than your skin and they stand erect. Your sag is real but your volume is greater. I don't like those who have perfect breasts in porn."

"Are you kidding me? Those are fake. Those girls all have boob jobs. Do you not know that?"

"Really? Didn't know. Turn over, Katrina. I want to see more of you in detail."

Katrina didn't need any encouragement to make herself the object of sexual examination. She flipped over and lay with her arms crossed under her face. "Look." She said and he did just that with the tips of his fingers canvassing over her butt.

"I never thought in my wildest dreams that this day would come. Even a few months ago, when we went for a swim, I was even thinking I would never see you again. And here you are naked and we just made love! Incredible!"

"Will you talk about this and boast to your friends that this happened?"

"Of course, not. How can I do that? It's so embarrassing to talk about stuff like that."

"Oh really? That's not what I hear. Men like to brag about the women they made love to."

"That's bullshit. Not one of my friends has talked about anything like it."

"Promise me that you won't tell anyone about what happened today."

"I swear I won't utter a word. And you? You won't tell?"

"Of course, I won't. I have more to lose than you. If I hear anything from anybody I will deny it and say I was forced."

"Ok."

# CHAPTER TEN

Giri continued his critical appraisal of the most beautiful woman on the planet. He had his eyes on every millimeter of Katrina's derriere; his fingertips absorbed its silky smoothness and softness. He had a desire to taste and he did. He started licking her on the side of her hips and slowly climbed the ample mound of her buttocks and finally parted her voluptuous cheeks and touched the skin around her asshole.

Minutes later, Giri held his penis and brought it in full view. Katrina reached to fondle it and play with his balls. "These become so beautiful when making love."

"Am I big enough to satisfy? I know you'll say it whatever but it matters to me."

"Size doesn't matter at all. Technique does. Making a woman feel special with gentleness matters. Some men are so big they hurt the woman."

"Aha, Katrina. Have you been with men who hurt you?" Giri giggled.

"Jeez, you are so obsessed with my experiences. No, I haven't."

"Turn over. I want to see your pussy again."

Katrina complied. "Why do they call it that?"

"Maybe because it is hairy like a pussycat. Why? You don't like it?"

"I guess I like cunt better. It is more raw. Pussy sounds like a nickname." Katrina giggled. "Do you like it shaved? Nowadays people don't like natural."

"How do you know this stuff when you are alone all these years?"

"Oh, my gosh. I have girl friends who are married for god's sake." Katrina found it difficult to look Giri in the eye. A tiny bit of guilt compelled her to explain more. "There's this good friend of mine who said her hubby liked her natural when they got married and now he wants her to shave."

"Yeah, all the porn stars are shaved. But I like it like yours." He looked right at her pussy.

Katrina parted her thighs slightly to give him a good view.

"Can I kiss you?"

She nodded.

Giri went down on Katrina again, licking her entire pubic area, not missing a millimeter then moving into her crack and the fixed his lips against her and sucked. Then, he touched her clit lightly and rotated his tongue on the little piece of flesh and then sucked again.

Katrina bucked in excitement. "Who taught you that? Give me your dick. It's time for me to suck it."

Giri turned slightly and pushed his dick towards her. Almost as soon as Katrina's slender fingers curled around his penis, she had him in her mouth. Giri gasped and then arched to feel the complete goodness; the exquisite feel of buccal mucosa on genital skin; the delicious touch of the tongue and teeth; the incredible sensation of low pressure. Just when Giri had thought that he had felt it all, he felt something new. Katrina drew him in and out exerting the correct amount pressure with her lips. Her hands went down to caress his balls as if they were precious, delicate fancies.

"Oh my god, please don't stop. Please..."

Katrina took it out of her mouth momentarily. "Just eat me, Giri. Devour me!"

"Do you—?"

"Too many questions! Everybody—" She had to stop sucking him to answer.

"Sorry, sorry. Keep going."

And Katrina did.

As Giri sucked, flicked, licked and stroked her clit, Katrina was thrilled she was a writhing mess even as she brought Giri close to his third orgasm.

"Do you want to cum in my mouth or do you want to take me from behind?" Katrina gasped turning around.

"You want me to go in your ass?"

"No, doggy-style. You want to fuck me in there?"

"No, no. I don't fancy that much. It means I'll spread on all fours and you'll put your dick inside and stroke me." Katrina was already on all fours and Giri went behind to, first enjoy the view and then knelt behind her to enter.

"OK. So, this angle is bit different." Katrina adjusted herself, brought her hand between her thighs, found Giri's dick and then guided him in as both of them flexed their knees to obtain ideal union. No sooner was Giri in, he started ramming

Katrina with powerful strokes grabbing her ass and her boobs and was bit rough with unbridled horniness. She enjoyed his strokes as they hit deeper and slid past her G spot.

"You like this position?" Giri was curious.

"Oh, I love it any which way. Keep doing that. Don't slow down." Her voice turned high-pitched.

Giri went for Katrina with renewed vigour. He knew not where the sexual juices flowed from. It absolutely looked like his incredible responses came from loving someone whom he thought he loved and longed for. Drawing his mind back to living this unforgettable moment, Giri toyed with experimenting with other positions. He asked: "Can you get on top? Like those porn stars?"

"Gosh! Why? Are you not liking this? I'm loving it. But yes, we can. A few more minutes of this, please." Katrina brought her hand underneath to masturbate and started moaning and gasping. "Ooh... I'm about to cum. Let's me get on top."

Giri disengaged and lay on his back, expectant like a newlywed. Katrina squatted over him lined up her pussy over his love stick and then separated her lips again and held Giri's cock with her other hand to get him in. It was such a gloriously sight that Giri couldn't help but ask: "Wow, what a sight! Can I take a picture?"

"What? Are you crazy?"

"No, really. I want to remember this moment forever. We won't be seen, I promise. I'll only take below our waists." He giggled.

"You'll share it, I'm sure. So, no!"

"Please. It's for my me for this incredible night. I'll never show it to anyone. Promise, promise, promise!"

Katrina felt her defenses weakening again. Without saying anything, she removed her bangles and band that she was still wearing on her left ring finger. Those would be the only way someone would recognize her. "OK." She succumbed to the desire to please this guy.

Giri grabbed his phone from the bedside table and clicked a couple of shots of the pose that he loved most. "Can I video you fucking me?"

"No! That's not nice. Also, you'll be distracted. That's enough."

Giri obeyed as Katrina drew him in and then started riding him with precise movements of her hips. He was lifted to erotic heights again, not only by the awesome cream of his organ by her expert vaginal muscles but also by her sounds of enjoyment; a titillating mix of wordless moans, groans, grunts and gasps.

Giri made his feeble contributions by hoisting his dick tirelessly to meet her thrusts. Then he felts the torrents of ejaculation threaten again and he announced it.

"Oh, I am cumming again. I am cumming!"

"Yes, pour into me. Cum! Give it all to me, you, big penis!" Katrina hadn't finished talking when Giri came into her with those jerks and she reciprocated with hers. She then collapsed on his chest moving downward to suck his manhood and lick the cum off every area of his genitals.

The clock struck one when the two cuddled to a slumber.

# CHAPTER ELEVEN

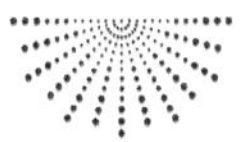

Giri squinted as the morning sun glinted through the curtains. He glanced at Katrina still a sleep turned away from him. The sheets hid her buttocks. He glanced at his watch and saw it was just past six.

He hopped out of bed and got dressed. He wondered if he could have a quickie, or even peep at Katrina's nakedness once more. He decided not to.

Giri went across, looked at her pretty sleeping face and kissed her cheek. She responded with a hum and an closed-eye smile.

"It's time to get up, sweetheart. Our train is coming in a couple of hours."

"Yeah, I know." She looked at him. "Oh, you're dressed already."

"We got to get moving. Don't know what the traffic is like at this hour."

"It's the weekend, silly. Did you enjoy our meeting last night?"

"Of course! I was forced!" Giri joked.

"Hmm. So, you won't tell anyone, right? Remember you promised."

"Promise."

Good heavens! All this woman thinks of is what other people will think!

"OK. See you in a few hours. I'll call you at 8." Giri then left.

* * *

The train journey back was not what Giri expected. He dreamed of intimacy with his brand-new lover. There were some men around and Katrina felt their prying eyes on her. Katrina and Giri had a good long chat before going to taking position in their respective areas.

"Why do you deny yourself so much and then pour out your passion so beautifully?" Giri whispered.

Katrina looked into his eyes to see if he would understand if she explained. "Women are different,

Giri. They are not ready to go all the time. They need time to get in the mood." She went on, in hushed tones, to share all she knew. He interrupted with innocent questions and Katrina explained as best as she could.

Katrina then switched up her tone and ended with this which took Giri aback: "Go and find a girl, Giri. You're a good guy. There are many out there waiting for you."

"We can't—we can't be together? What happened?"

Katrina grabbed his hand. "I have a life I have made for myself. I have a teenage son. I can't change those things. I hope you understand."

"Not even to meet once in a while? You know?"

"It will get complicated, Giri. Trust me. We'll get dependant on each other and then people will talk."

"Please, Katrina, sweetie. You made me so happy last night and you taught me so many things and actually made me a man."

"I really think we should end it here. It was good for you and me. You're a good lover. Girls will love you." She patted his cheek.

"I won't. It won't happen. You won't have pity

on me again if I'm lonely? I mean if I fuck someone else?"

Katrina looked sharply at him. "That's such a cheap way to look at it. It wasn't pity from me." Katrina may have been a bit untruthful. "And I'm not here to satisfy unfulfilled desires."

Giri had spoilt the whole thing with his insistent behavior.

When they parted to go their respective ways, there was naturally a bit of uneasiness.

A few days later, Giri tried reaching Katrina, first texting and then calling her but couldn't get through. He tried again after hour after hour and also sent an email message.

Still, there was no reply.

Giri tried all over again the next day, and again the same result. In the evening, he tried his luck again, with fears that she may be sick or something. He called a friend and she assured him Katrina was doing fine. When Giri gave himself a break for a few days, he called and texted again he was shocked to find out Katrina had done something that shattered his heart.

She had either changed her number or had blocked him! The email had no reply but it was valid. Giri just sat on his bed and cried.

He recollected every minute of their affair and decided to write it down, so as not to forget details.

A month later, Katrina did something she never did before. She was browsing some porn sites and after several pages under the 'Desi' section, she found what she feared all along. Two pictures under the caption, 'The Loner and the Widow'; in one, there was a woman squatting over a man, whose long penis she held. The fingers and the nail polish color were familiar. Her thighs were parted and her hairy vagina was partially open showing the inner lips and clit. The next was of perhaps the same woman facing away completely naked. The photo was blurred out around the head area.

It was her and Giri in the first picture. The bastard had posted the pictures after all. She didn't even know he had taken more than one. Katrina looked for the slightest signs of recognition. For half an hour or so, she examined it and saw there were no obvious signs. Even if there were, people would only speculate.

Then, Katrina looked at it through a man's eyes. She somehow felt proud of the way she looked. Her ass appeared so shapely and curvy. Her pussy was even more stunning; wet, creamy and reddish. The same one that held value in David who praised her for it.

Katrina looked so sexy and her pictures were enough that in two weeks of being posted, they had amassed over 4o0,000 views.

Giri did what most hurt men would have done if they couldn't have what they want. Yet, somehow, Katrina felt vindicated that she decided to scratch him off her life for good that day.